Ireland: January 1

Nowruz: around March 21 on the spring equinox

Zimbabwe:
January 1

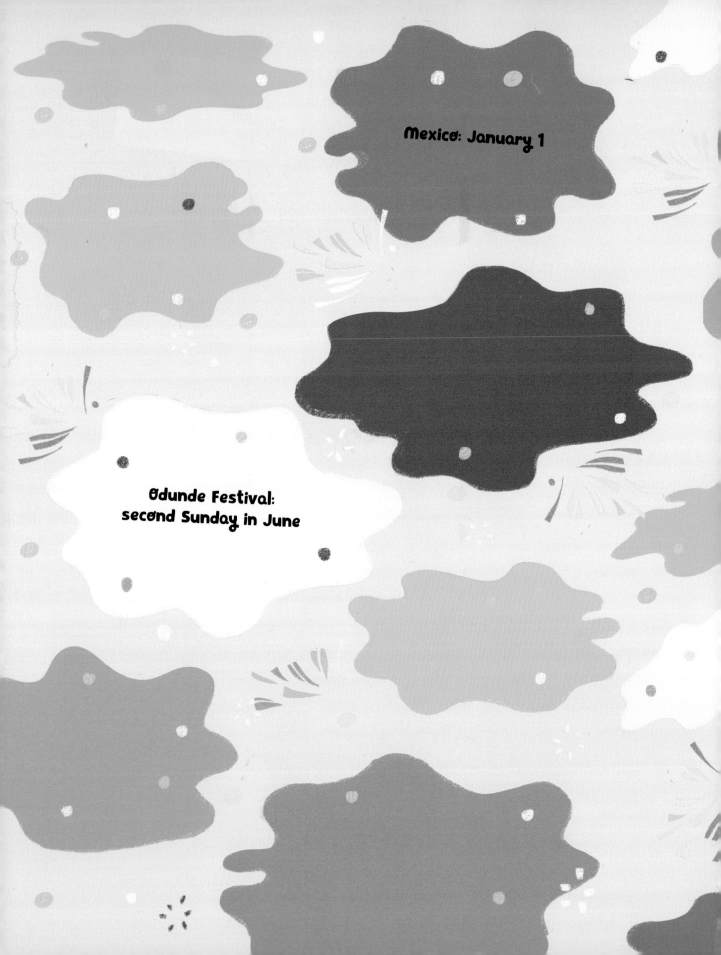

Mexico: January 1

Odunde Festival: second Sunday in June

A Year of Celebraciones

by Carrie Lara, PsyD

illustrated by
Christine Battuz

Magination Press · Washington, DC · American Psychological Association

To my friend Lauren who helped inspire the idea of using New Year's in the story, and all my friends and family for sharing their traditions with me—*CL*

To my friend Catou, to all those beautiful moments we share—*CB*

Magination Press
Books for Kids From the
American Psychological Association

Magination Press is a registered trademark of the American Psychological Association. Order books at maginationpress.org, or call 1-800-374-2721.

Book design by Gwen Grafft
Printed by Sonic Media Solutions, Inc., Medford, NY

Cataloging-in-Publication is available at the Library of Congress.

ISBN: 978-1-4338-4155-2
eISBN: 978-1-4338-4156-9

Manufactured in the United States of America
10 9 8 7 6 5 4 3 2 1

Do you ever wonder about other people?

My mom told me that no two snowflakes are alike.
And that people, families, and cultures
are like that too.

All around us people live in different homes and neighborhoods,

speak beautiful languages,

eat yummy foods,

and have unique traditions.

My friend Lizette's family is from Mexico and speaks Spanish sometimes, just like we do. And Kham's family is from Laos and speaks Laotian.

In mi familia I have dos culturas and me encanta learning about them. They are what help make mi, me!

In school we learned about New Year's celebrations. Everyone brought something from their family traditions to present.

I love New Year's and I couldn't wait to share with my friends!

Thomas went first. "My grandparents are Scottish," he said, "and on New Year's in their village they make balls out of wire and fill them with sticks and hay. Then they light the balls on fire and throw them into the lake!

They said that watching me play with sparklers reminds them of this tradition."

"In the Lao tradition for New Year's," Kham shared, "we wash everything with water perfumed with flowers. After we are done washing, my sisters and brothers and I throw the water at each other for fun!"

She showed us a silk flower called a Dok Champa.

"Persian New Year is called Nowruz," said Ahmad. "We make a haftseen table, set with seven things that start with the letter S, like sabzeh—sprouts.

At the end of the 13 days of celebration my family puts some of the stuff from the Nowruz table in a river. The water washes away the old and starts everything fresh."

"My family is Chinese," said Mei, "and we celebrate the new year on the new moon between January 21st and February 20th."

Mei passed around a hongbao, a red envelope with gold symbols and money inside. "To be polite we pass it using both hands."

I didn't know people celebrated New Year's at different times of year, and for whole weeks or more!

"The Jewish New Year is called Rosh Hashanah," said Lauren. "It's usually in September and is the first two days of a 10 day celebration of the High Holidays, ending on Yom Kippur." She held up a horn. "This is my shofar. It's a special horn that is blown during certain prayers at the synagogue."

"We throw breadcrumbs in the river to wash away the old. Each year I talk with my parents about the mistakes I learned from last year and what I want to work on to do better."

Kaila held up a cloth with vibrant colors. "I got this when I visited my aunt last summer in Philadelphia. She took me to a festival called Odunde.

It comes from the New Year tradition of the Yoruba people of Nigeria. There were lots of booths with food, art, and clothing, celebrating the cultures of Africans, African Americans, and Caribbean Africans.

My favorite part was the parade to the river where they offered fruit and flowers to Oshun, goddess of the river," Kaila said.

So many ways to celebrate the same holiday! And we had so much in common, too. Food was a big deal for everybody.

I love eating cinnamon rolls and egg casserole on New Year's morning while we watch the Rose Parade.

Lauren's family eats sweet apples dipped in honey and round bread called challah.

Mei's family eats noodles to represent a long life, and dumplings for wealth.

Lizette has soup on New Year's Day made from the bag of lentils her family leaves on the porch the night before for good fortune.

Our teacher Mr. Ramirez is from Spain, and his family eats 12 grapes at midnight with the chimes of the clock. "There's a special trick to it so you don't miss a single one," he said.

"Dong – grape!
Dong – grape!"
The whole class giggled.

"In Nicaragua they eat grapes on New Year's Eve too, but we've never done it with the clock," I told Mr. Ramirez. "It sounds fun!"

Finally, it was my turn!

My dad is from Nicaragua, and they make un año viejo, which is an old man or woman made of stuffed clothes. At midnight they light it on fire to burn away the old year and welcome the new one."

I held up a stuffed sock that had doll clothes and a face drawn on it. "In mi familia, we make a smaller año viejo that we put in the backyard firepit after we watch the ball drop and fireworks on TV."

After everyone shared their family traditions,
we created a mural with our symbols.
We painted fireworks all around because
everyone agreed that fireworks are awesome!

There was Thomas' ball made of chicken wire and dried grass, Ahmad's sabzeh, Lauren's shofar, Mei's hongbao, Kaila's cloth, Mr. Ramirez's grapes, Lizette's bag of lentils, Kham's Dok Champa flower, and mi año viejo was pinned in the middle.

When we were done, we took a picture to put on the school website. I felt so proud. I learned so much about myself and my friends. I can't wait to learn more!

Our mural shows us all connected in celebración.
There's room for everyone in this mundo maravilloso!

Reader's Note

"We must learn about other cultures in order to understand, in order to love, and in order to preserve our common world heritage."–Yo Yo Ma

A Year of Celebraciones follows a young girl's continuing cultural education as she learns about the many ways her classmates celebrate the new year. She is eager to share her own family's cultural traditions with her friends in the class assignment, and is pleasantly surprised to learn about her classmates' traditions. Some kids celebrate on December 31 and January 1 like she does, and some celebrate at other times of the year. She discovers that holidays are full of traditions, and that there is room for everyone's culture in the class mural.

How Do Children Develop Cultural Identity?

Cultural identity development is a process that begins right away when a child is born. "Cultural identity" refers to a sense of belonging to a particular group and includes the traditions, language, religion, music, food, ancestry, thinking patterns, and social structures of a culture.

Children are little social scientists, learning from their observations and experiences within their families and communities. In the first stage the developmental focus is on "the self," who they are in the context of their environment.

Children start to notice difference between physical features as early as 6 months of age, and they start to identify their own cultural identity around the age of 3-4 years with the development of more complex language. This identification comes from the interactions they have with their family members, friends, teachers, and community. Race is a social construct and is an aspect of cultural identity. By age 7-9, children are more aware of the group dynamics around culture and race. This includes the histories of their own culture, and how they are similar, different, or a combination of cultures together. In my other two picture books featuring this character, *Marvelous Maravilloso: Me and My Beautiful Family* and *The Heart of Mi Familia*, I highlight this process.

In *Marvelous Maravilloso* the little girl takes us through the beauty she sees in the colors of the world around her, including the diverse colors of people. In *The Heart of Mi Familia*, she shares the similarities and differences between her grandmother's and her abuela's home, and how they come together in her own bicultural family. "In my home, two worlds become one," she tells us. *A Year of Celebraciones* follows the same girl as she continues to grow. She has come to the next stage where she is learning about "the other." In cultural identity theory, the idea is that in learning about others we learn more about ourselves. We connect with others and explore our differences, understanding how we relate within the larger community based on cultural norms and social constructs.

Creating Opportunities to Learn

It is important to continue having conversations about culture, race, and diversity with our children as they grow and develop. This book provides a springboard for developing a conversation, but there are so many opportunities. Ask your child what cultures interest them. Follow their lead and plan a visit to a museum for art or history of that culture. Observe with your child the culture in the exhibits or vice versa the art and history in the culture! Be creative. There are so many ways to learn about your own and other cultures and promote an attitude of curiosity. Here are a few more to get you started.

- Listen to music from around the world. This introduces new languages, different musical stylistic compositions, and beats.
- Dance! Another easy way to learn about a new culture is to look up a traditional or popular dance and learn some steps. Often dance tells us stories about the history of culture and traditions.
- Learn a children's game from another culture and play with your child and their friends.
- Who doesn't love food? Look up a restaurant in your area that serves dishes from the cuisine of another culture and read about the food offered before going to try some.
- Research a traditional recipe from another culture and prepare it at home. Where did it come from? What are the cultural ties? Now go ahead and cook it up to enjoy! You could even have a potluck with friends to share the different dishes, both the history and to eat!

- Pick a craft from another culture you'd like to learn about and try it out.
- Learn how to say *hello*, *goodbye*, and *thank you* in multiple languages.
- Attend a cultural festival in your area.
- Research the different money types around the world. Maybe play a game with play money you can create, pretending to be a world market.

Many Ways to Celebrate

In the story of *A Year of Celebraciones*, I was only able to capture a handful of cultures and one or two of their new year's traditions. In researching this book, I had the wonderful opportunity to learn about so many more, and I wish I could have included every single one of them! However, I hope that this small taste leaves you in a place of wanting to continue to learn more. Perhaps there's something about your own family's celebrations around the new year you want to learn more about. Or perhaps you have friends or neighbors that have different traditions than your family and you want to learn about them. Or maybe your child's teacher does, or the new kid in class. I encourage you to take action, and explore the world around you and all the amazing cultures you can learn about.

Carrie Lara, PsyD, is a licensed clinical psychologist who has worked with a range of clients, from children and families to adults with severe mental illness. She is an award-winning children's book author whose books include *Marvelous Maravilloso*, *The Heart of Mi Familia*, and *Out of the Fires*. She lives in Sonoma County, CA with her family. Visit carriealara.com and @AuthorCarrieLara on Facebook and Instagram.

Christine Battuz has illustrated over 60 children's books, including *Marvelous Maravilloso*, *The Heart of Mi Familia*, *My Sister Beth's Pink Birthday*, and *Shy Spaghetti and Excited Eggs*. Her work appears in educational books, magazines, toys, and toy packaging. She teaches art to adults and children of all ages. She lives in Bromont, Quebec. Visit her at mbArtists.com and illustrationquebec.com.

Magination Press is the children's book imprint of the American Psychological Association. It's the combined power of psychology and literature that makes a Magination Press book special. Visit maginationpress.org and @MaginationPress on Facebook, Twitter, Instagram, and Pinterest.

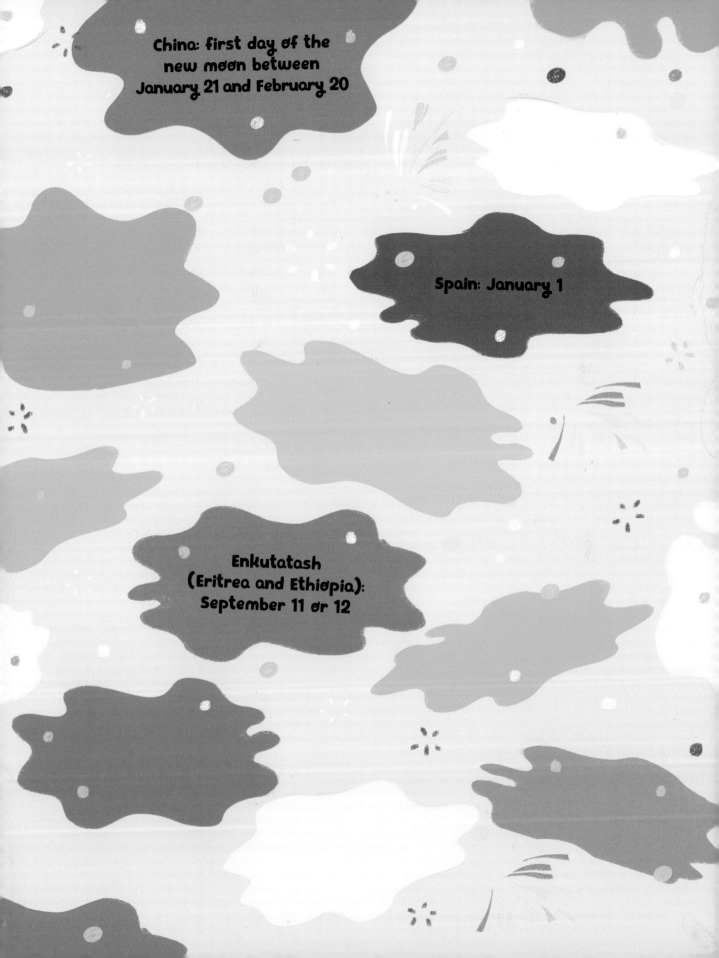

China: first day of the
new moon between
January 21 and February 20

Spain: January 1

Enkutatash
(Eritrea and Ethiopia):
September 11 or 12

South Africa:
January 1

Rosh Hashanah: celebrated
for two days, usually in the
month of September.

Ghaaji (Navajo New Year):
October